This book belongs to . . .

www.makebelieveideas.com

Written by Rosie Greening.
Illustrated by Lara Ede.

The VERY hungry WORRY MONSTERS

Lara Ede · Rosie Greening

make believe ideas

Hi! I'm Frettie Fluster.
I don't want to boast, but I am a **WORRY MONSTER** expert.
I know absolutely _everything_ about . . .

...WHAT DO YOU MEAN, "WHAT'S A WORRY MONSTER?"

Honestly, what are parents teaching their kids these days?

It's lucky you found me!

I can tell you **everything** about these **friendly** fluffballs.
Guess what the **WORRY MONSTERS** eat.

Not pizza.

Not
burgers.

WORRIES!

Humans don't like having worries.
But they make a
munchtastic meal
for the WORRY MONSTERS.

Let´s meet them!

This is WORRIED-ABOUT-BATHS MONSTER.

If bath time gets you in a lather, he´s your guy!

He eats the worry,

GOBBLE-CRUNCH-MUNCH!

After that, taking a bath is
easy-peasy-monster-squeezy.

This is SCARED-OF-THE-DARK MONSTER!
She stops you from worrying about things in the dark.

B-b-big things with g-g-glowing eyes...

...S-S-S-Scared-of-the-Dark Monster?

Are you there?

PHEW! There she is.
I wasn't worried, were you?

There's a WORRY MONSTER for all kinds of worries!
Like SCARED-OF-SNOTTY-SNEEZES MONSTER.

AH-
AH-
AH-ACHOOOOOOOO!

But you haven't seen my favourite WORRY MONSTER yet.

I can't wait for you to meet her!

Is she down here?

Excuse me, FEAR-OF-QUESTIONS MONSTER.

Have you seen my favourite worry monster?

2 + 2 = 4.

The Eiffel Tower.

Roughly 486 llamas.

That word reversed is MOTTOB.

There were no unicorns on Old MacDonald's farm.

Farting at school.

Oh no. He has all the answers except the one I need!

Let's ask WORRIED-ABOUT-RUMBLY-TUMMIES MONSTER.
He's useful if feeling hungry gets you in a stew.

Excuse me, have you seen my favourite worry monster?

No, that's a pineapple.

No, that's a sandwich.

Never mind.

Ah, my favourite **WORRY MONSTER** must be hiding behind a door!

No.

No.

No.

Nope.

Not you.

Absolutely not.

Oh no, no, no!
My favourite WORRY MONSTER is LOST! And I'm . . .

I need to **remember** my **worry training.**

calm down.

Take a deep breath.

Think of fluffy puppies.

Write down the worry . . . .

. . .and put it **safely** in my **rucksack** for a **WORRY MONSTER** to eat.

?

Wait, what's in here?

IT'S MY FAVOURITE WORRY MONSTER!

I put her in there
so she wouldn't
get lost.

Can you **guess** what she's called?

She's the

Worried-About-

WORRYING

MONSTER!

Now we can STOP worrying and have some FUN.

Trust me... I'm a WORRY-MONSTER expert!

FEAR-OF-THE-STORY-ENDING MONSTER...